Adriana's Quest

THE BIRTH OF THE TOOTH FAIRY

KEVIN L. MCQUAID

ILLUSTRATIONS BY
KRISTEN CAMISA

THANKSGIVING

Kevin M. says: Special thanks be to Debra R., who believed, and Cemantha C., who inspired and helped in so many ways. Thanks be as well to Autumn M., who went above & beyond. M and M: I love U IXI.

Kristen C. says: Thanks to my teachers at Ringling College of Art + Design for their excellent instruction and advice, my friends for their constant encouragement and inspiration, and my family for their love, guidance, and support.

Adriana's Quest | The Birth of the Tooth Fairy
Copyright 2016 by Kevin L. McQuaid
Text copyright 2016 by Kevin L. McQuaid. Illustration copyright 2016 by Kayelem Publishing LLC.
All rights reserved. Printed in the United States of America.
ISBN: 978-1540856500
Library of Congress Control Number: 2016920320
CreateSpace Independent Publishing Platform, North Charleston, S.C.

❀

Library of Congress Cataloging-In-Publication Data
McQuaid, Kevin L.
Adriana's Quest | The Birth of the Tooth Fairy/ By Kevin L. McQuaid – 1st ed
Summary: To help a group of squirrels and defeat an enemy, a fairy collects human teeth and becomes the Tooth Fairy.
[1. Fairies – fiction.   2. Adventure – fiction.   3. Fantasy – fiction
4. Teeth – fiction.

❀

Book design by Autumn Musick

Adriana's Quest

THE BIRTH OF THE TOOTH FAIRY

For my parents and Robin Manners,
the best teacher a young writer could ever want

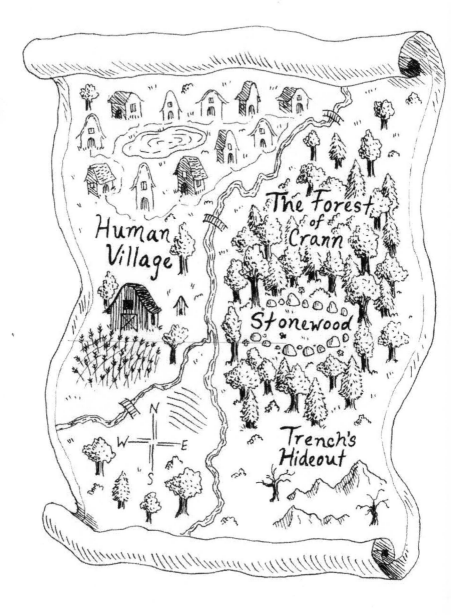

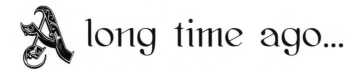

ONE: THE BLACK SQUIRRELS

The Black Squirrels had been our friends forever.

We fairies of Stonewood Village helped them find nuts in winter, played games with them, and watched their young grow old. They, in turn, watched over us and made sure we were safe anywhere we went in the Forest of Crann, which was all around our village.

One cold night, just after a frost, the chief of the Black Squirrels limped into Stonewood. He looked hurt.

We gathered around him. Kliren rose up on his hind legs and stood, a small pine cone taller than we were. His big, dark eyes looked sad. When he opened his mouth, we saw why: His top two front teeth were gone.

He said he and the other squirrels had woken up from sleep wrapped in spider's webs. All their front teeth were taken.

"Watch, and be careful," he said, before leaving us in his inchworm way, hopping and then pausing every few twig lengths to stand and sniff the air.

I looked about. Every fairy from our village looked afraid, even the olders.

I was scared, too, so I tried thinking about something fun, like the games my best friend, Adriana, and I did together. We always had a great time playing "airflip," a flying chase game. One of us would fly headlong into a tree hole, flip around, and go back out. A second player would follow and try to touch the other before they got past.

The first flyer won an acorn if they didn't get touched. Adriana was really good at it, because she could bend so well and was smaller than most fairies our age.

We also played Sdrawkcab, a game in which we said words backwards. Adriana became "Anairda," tree became "eert," bird became "drib." The olders looked at us funny and shook their heads when we talked that way, and that made us laugh.

But it was no time for games, I knew.

Even Olcas, Stonewood's chief and the keeper of our fairy magic, looked upset. He walked around the village with his hands behind his back talking to himself, like he often did when he needed to think.

No fairy in Stonewood could imagine why the squirrels' teeth would have been taken from them. But we soon found out.

Two: Red Trench Comes Calling

Redanthan Trench flew into Stonewood during the whole moon after Kliren's visit. With him came an icy wind that made us shiver. Adriana and I stood very close together.

He bowed hello and ran a hand through his long, black beard as he twitched his fairy wings. He spoke of a new enemy in the Forest of Crann.

"Giants," Trench said. "They want all the trees. But we can stop them – together. I have a group of animals willing to help us. If you do not join me, you will end up far worse than the squirrels, whose teeth I took to warn you. There will be no more Stonewood, I promise you, if the giants get their way.

"I will give you three full moons to join with me," he said before flying away. "Three moons!"

We all began talking about the new enemy. Hearing

the noise, Olcas came out of his tree just then, yawning and scratching his white beard. When we told him what had happened, he frowned, and told us Trench was a fairy known to be friends with snakes and rats and bugs — and even crows!

Olcas knew a lot, because he had lived many winters – all the way back to the Age of One, when fairy and elf and human and beast lived all together before the Great Divide split everyone up and most humans stopped believing in magic.

He started walking around with his hands behind his back again.

Adriana seemed even more afraid than I was. She was trembling, and looked like she was about to cry. But to be fair, she looked like that a lot and was scared

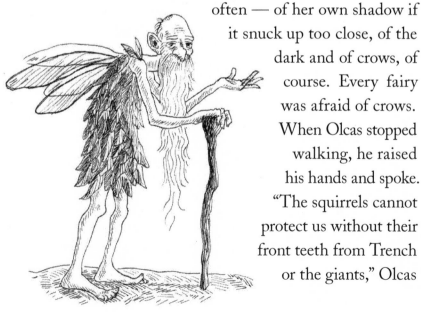

often — of her own shadow if it snuck up too close, of the dark and of crows, of course. Every fairy was afraid of crows. When Olcas stopped walking, he raised his hands and spoke. "The squirrels cannot protect us without their front teeth from Trench or the giants," Olcas said. "I don't think there's anything we can do, except … except join Trench."

The olders gasped.

"No. No!"

Olcas shook his head, and he and his young helper, Valandoor, who stood quietly behind him as always, flew off.

Adriana went about a branch length away and knelt on the ground. She was bent over, drawing with a finger in the dirt.

I flew over and stood behind her. She sat up straight, still on her knees, and turned toward me. To my surprise, she didn't look afraid at all.

"Olcas said there's nothing we can do but join Trench," she said. "But I know something we can do."

Adriana wanted to get the squirrels new teeth.

"What if we went round the forest and asked animals for spare teeth?" she asked Olcas.

"Well..." Olcas said, crossing his arms in front of him the way olders sometimes did. "You couldn't just put another animal's teeth into a squirrel's mouth. They wouldn't fit."

He was right. The squirrels' front teeth were different from any other animal we knew: They were thick, and strong.

Adriana looked to the ground, as if Olcas had asked some great riddle no fairy knew the answer to, like why the moon grew then shrank in the sky, or why rain came.

"But mustn't we try something?" Adriana asked.

Olcas chuckled.

"Oh, all right," he said. "Go ahead and try. But don't be surprised if no animal in Crann is willing to give you their teeth."

Adriana fetched a satchel of leaves tied together from her tree and slipped it over her shoulder.

"What are you doing?" I asked.

"Going," she said.

"Going? Where?"

She pointed.

"Beyond the village?" I said. "But, it's getting dark."

"I know," Adriana said, swallowing hard. "But there aren't many moons until the third full moon, until we'll have to join Trench and fight the giants. There has to be another way."

I was about to mention that crows would be about, but I stopped myself.

"Then I'm going with you," I said. That made Adriana smile.

We touched wings — a fairy promise to help one another — and flew off. We were both scared. Neither of us had ever been outside Stonewood before.

Olcas warned us about trouble, and it wasn't long before trouble found us and Adriana found herself deep inside the mouth of a fox.

Adriana said she had a great idea for how to collect teeth. I thought about reminding her of how she'd once had a great idea to pet a skunk, too, and how that hadn't turned out so well, but I kept quiet.

"We could ask chickens," she said. "They're friendly, at least I think they are, and if not, we could just fly away. We've got to be faster than any chicken."

We spotted a human farm about a sunbeam's length away from Stonewood, on the edge of the forest, and flew down. The first streaks of light were beginning to poke through the dark.

The hens' house was small, with a kind of metal covering over the windows and the door. We could hear them chattering inside.

Now I was shaking. Fairies were told never, ever to get near humans or where they lived.

"I don't know about this, Adriana."

"Emoc no!," she said, stamping her foot. "It's still mostly dark, so we'll be safe."

Adriana bent back the door's metal covering and stepped inside. The chickens squawked.

"No, no, quiet! Please!" she said.

The chickens were sitting on nests on wooden planks.

In a herky-jerky motion, one bent her head and turned an eye toward us.

"Our village needs help," Adriana began, speaking fast. "A bad fairy hurt our squirrel friends by stealing their teeth."

The hens gasped.

"'Tis true," Adriana said. "So we're out looking for new teeth for them. Do you have any you could spare?"

The chickens began to cluck and giggle, until they were laughing hard and jerking their heads all about.

"What?" Adriana said, puzzled.

One of the hens stopped giggling long enough to speak.

"We don't mean to laugh at you, it's just that ... you don't understand ... as everyone knows..."

Adriana and I leaned in closer.

"We don't have teeth!" the chicken said.

Then they all howled with laughter. Adriana's wings drooped. We flew off in silence and let the wind carry us.

When the sun came fully out, we saw a fox sniffing the ground near a clump of trees. His fur was dark red and brown and white, and his nose very black.

We decided to fly down and ask him for teeth. Foxes ate fairies, we'd been told, so we stayed a branch length away, to be safe.

"Well, hello, hello," said the fox. "And what brings you two sprites out of the forest, hmm?"

"I am Adriana of Stonewood, and we are on a quest,"

she said, as bravely as she could.

"On a journey you say? Hmmm."

"Yes, and we need some teeth."

"Teeth, you say?"

We took turns telling him the whole tale, and he listened with his pink tongue dripping out of his mouth.

"I happen to have two teeth in the back of my mouth that are quite loose," he said. "I'd be happy to help you."

"I would be most gentle in removing them, sir," Adriana said.

"My name is Gramaldagan," he replied, bowing. "My friends call me Gram."

And with that he sat down on his back legs, closed his eyes and opened his mouth wide.

Adriana tip-toed toward him, picking up a small stick along the way. She flew up and peered inside his mouth. His teeth were sharp, and his mouth bigger than any either of us had ever seen.

"You won't hurt me, will you?" Gram said, sounding scared.

Adriana crawled inside the fox's mouth for a look, then quickly backed out again and gently put the stick upright before returning to where Gram said his loose teeth were. All I could see of her were the bottoms of her feet. I held my breath.

"Anairda," I said, speaking backwards. "Luferac!"

The fox gave me a strange look. Adriana called out

in a muffled voice from inside his mouth.

"There aren't any loose ones," she huffed.

"You're right about that, my breakfast!"

With that, the fox tried to clamp his jaws shut. I closed my eyes.

When I opened them, Adriana was beside me. The stick had kept him from biting down on her.

"You tricked me," he yelled, shaking the stick from his mouth. "Me!"

"You were going to eat me, Gramaldagan!" Adriana said, pointing a finger at the fox. "Shame on you."

We flew off. I could tell Adriana was upset we hadn't gotten any teeth, and that she'd nearly been breakfast.

"Maybe Olcas was right," I said. "Animals won't just give us teeth."

"But there has to be some creature about that has extra teeth they don't need," Adriana said.

Five: Timber

When we got back home to Stonewood, we told Olcas everything that had happened. He seemed surprised that we were back so soon.

As we were telling him our story, though, we heard a loud crashing sound at the edge of the forest.

It made the whole ground shake, and we could hear voices — human voices.

Olcas' eyes bulged, and he flew toward the noise. Adriana and I followed, making sure to hide behind rocks and trees so we wouldn't be seen.

Where the trees met the grass, we saw a group of humans standing around a tree lying on the ground. They held long metal tools in their hands.

They seemed rather happy. Two of the older humans tied a kind of vine to the tree.

"This is good timber, Murphy," one said.

Beside them, a group of smaller humans jumped about, playing. They didn't seem to care whether the tree was up or down.

Adriana and I stared from behind a rock. Neither of us had ever seen a human before. We had always been told humans were awful creatures, but these didn't seem to be too bad.

"There's wood aplenty here," the one they called Murphy said, as they dragged the tree away.

When they were gone, Olcas turned to us.

"This is why Red Trench wants us to join him," he said, a deep frown on his face. "Humans are the giants, the enemy."

"Because they took a tree?" Adriana said.

"No. Because they will take the whole forest. Someday, if they keep cutting down trees, this whole wood will be gone — and so will our village, and our food, everything. This is why we can never be friends with humans."

Olcas shook his head and began to fly away.

Adriana stared after the humans as they walked back to their own village. The smallest ones were riding on top of the tree, laughing, as it was dragged. They didn't look like any enemy.

Adriana's face suddenly brightened.

"Olcas!" she called out. "Didn't you tell us once that young humans lose their teeth before they are full grown?"

"No, Adriana," Olcas said. "You can't be around humans for any reason — ever!"

"But if human teeth fall out when they are young, I could gather them up while they slept. We could then melt them down and reshape them for the squirrels. And the moon is almost full again, and soon Trench will return. Please, I have to try."

Olcas took in a long breath.

"Allright," he said finally. "But you need to wait a bit. There may be something I can do to help you to be safer in the human world."

Olcas spent the next few suns and moons in his tree, hammering and cooking up potions we could smell from a long way off.

When he came out, he was carrying a shiny necklace, with three round stones in it.

One of the stones was a milky pink. Another was a creamy blue; it looked like the sky. In the middle, slightly larger than the other two, was a bright purple stone that sparkled like the water when the sun hit it.

Olcas held up the necklace, walked up to Adriana and went behind her.

A crowd gathered. Olcas put the necklace around her

neck and fastened it. When he did, the stones glowed. The crowd whispered.

Adriana touched the necklace softly, and smiled.

"This is a Necklace of Secrets," Olcas said. "Touch the pink stone."

Adriana tapped the stone and it buzzed softly.

"That stone will buzz like a bee when you are near a human tooth that has fallen out," Olcas said. "Now the blue one. Touch it."

Adriana tapped a finger on it, and it, too, shook gently.

"That one will buzz if a human child is asleep, and buzz a second time if a child wakes up when you are near."

Adriana smiled wider.

"Now, for the purple one in the center," Olcas said. "Touch it, please."

Adriana touched the stone and disappeared. A gasp rang out from the crowd. Olcas smiled.

"How do you feel, Adriana?"

"Fine."

Another gasp.

"And you can see us then?"

"Of course I can."

"But we cannot see you at all," Olcas said. "Humans won't be able to, either. Now, touch the purple stone again, Adriana."

In an eyeblink, she was standing exactly as before. The fairies in the crowd clapped their wings together in delight. Adriana threw her arms around Olcas and hugged him as tightly as she could.

"Here, take this as well," Olcas said, handing her a small sack with green dust in it. "A few grains will put human or animal or fairy to sleep right away."

"Thanks be to you," Adriana said. "I'll wear the necklace and take the dust with me tonight, when I go to the human village yonder where those dragged the tree. Soon we'll have all the human teeth we need to help the squirrels!"

I told Adriana I wanted to go with her.

"You'll need a lookout," I said. "And what if you get a lot of teeth? You won't be able to carry them all by yourself."

She thought for a bit. "Well, it would be nice to have a friend along – and a lookout."

The night was chilly, but the moonlight made it easy to see. We glided into the human village, just beyond where we had met the chickens. All was quiet.

After a while we found a window — Olcas had told us all about human houses — that was cracked open.

Adriana touched the necklace's pink stone, but nothing happened. At the fourth house we came upon, the pink stone buzzed. Adriana put a finger to the blue stone. It also buzzed, meaning a child was asleep.

She crawled through an open window, and then pointed to a large lump underneath piles of cloth. I saw her tap the purple stone, and disappear.

Adriana found the human child's tooth laying on top of the cloth pile and came back outside smiling, holding it as if it were the last ripe berry before winter set in. She carefully placed it inside her satchel.

By then, light was poking through the night. Though

we were tired, Adriana wanted to try one more human house — one bigger than all the others around it, sitting by itself up a long, winding lane.

Inside, she would meet a girl human who would change everything about her quest.

Eight: Morgan

Adriana touched the purple stone and started looking for a tooth on the girl's bed. Even with the moonlight, she couldn't find one. She sat down to think.

"What are you doing here?" the girl suddenly asked.

Adriana froze. The blue stone hadn't buzzed a second time.

"What's your name?" the girl asked.

"This human cannot see me," Adriana told herself. "I just need to stay still."

"My name is Morgan," the girl said. "I've never seen a real fairy before. Can you hear me? Can you speak?"

Adriana stayed very still, but her mind was racing. Seen a fairy?

Adriana swallowed hard. She was just a few leaf-lengths away from an actual human! Although she was very scared, the girl's voice seemed very kind.

"I am Adriana," she said.

"That's a beautiful name," Morgan said, rising up to her elbows. "Why are you here?"

"I...I came to collect your tooth."

"You mean this one?" Morgan sat up and opened her mouth, wiggling a loose tooth back and forth.

"Yes, I think so. How can you see me?" Adriana asked.

"Because you're right in front of me," Morgan said, shrugging.

Adriana began to feel afraid again. She knew she shouldn't be talking to a human. She thought about flying back out of the window.

"Why do you want my tooth?" Morgan asked.

"You, you promise you won't hurt me?"

"I promise," Morgan said.

Adriana thought it might be a trick. But she decided to take a chance.

"A bad fairy wants our village to help defeat what he says is an enemy, and I am on a quest to help our friends the Black Squirrels so we don't have to join him," she said.

"Well, I'll help you," Morgan said, tugging at her tooth. "We might need some string to, ah, hold on – there!"

She pulled the tooth out of her mouth and held it up. Adriana didn't move.

"Oh, I see. I don't trust strangers, either," Morgan said. "That's smart. Here."

She reached over and placed the tooth on a pillow. Without taking her eyes off the girl, Adriana grabbed the tooth and flew up to the ceiling. Morgan giggled.

"How long have you been doing this?" she asked.

"This is my first moon among humans," Adriana said.

"And how many teeth have you gotten?"

"Just two," Adriana said.

"I don't have any more loose teeth right now," Morgan said. "But I'll give you all mine when they come out if you'd like."

"Will it take long? I've only two full moons left."

"I could tell my friends. There are many children in this village, and I bet they'd be happy to help you, too."

"You would do that — for me?"

"Why not?" Morgan asked.

"Well, with the Great Divide — "

"The what?"

Adriana could tell by the sound of her voice that Morgan had never heard of the Great Divide. She changed the subject.

"Why do human teeth fall out?"

21

Morgan yawned a little yawn and nestled down in her bed.

"Can I tell you about teeth some other time? I have to get back to sleep now," Morgan said. "It's almost morning."

"Ok. Thank you for the tooth," Adriana said.

"You're welcome," Morgan said, yawning again. "I'll spread the word about your quest to my friends. Please come back and see me soon and we'll get you more teeth."

Adriana smiled, flew to the window and crawled through.

"With Morgan's help, we'll have all the teeth we need before the next full moon!" Adriana said to me. "I can't wait to tell Olcas!"

A bird's flight away, though, Red Trench was telling his helper Sephian, his snakes and his crows that a Stonewood fairy was trying to get teeth from the human village to help the squirrels - and that she had to be stopped.

NINE: PILLOWS

We saw Morgan again two sundowns later.

"We have a problem," Adriana said.

"We?" Morgan asked, still half asleep.

"Well, yes, I have a friend," I could hear her say from outside the window.

"Could I meet her, too?"

Adriana gestured for me to come inside. I said hello and told Morgan my name.

"I need one place in every child's house where I can find their teeth after they've come out," Adriana said. "It'll take too long to find them otherwise. And it needs to be somewhere a human child can put them."

Morgan thought.

"Every house is different," she said. "I can't think of anyplace!"

With that she flopped backwards, her head landing in a thud on her pillow.

"Hey…" Adriana said.

We all looked at each other, and smiled. From that point on, we knew from where Adriana would collect teeth.

Ten: Trading

Morgan told all her friends what to do when their teeth came out, and word of the quest spread among the children in her village. Each night, Adriana would gather them from under their pillows.

The moon grew bright, and full, then darkened again.

Every few suns, a human would come and chop down another tree from our forest. Whenever they did, Olcas would get very quiet.

As we flew back to Stonewood one night after gathering teeth, Adriana and I began talking about the village children.

"They're giving us teeth," I said. "Shouldn't we give them something in return?"

Adriana thought.

"I don't know what we could give to humans," she said. "Except…"

We asked Morgan the next time we saw her.

"We don't know enough about you humans to know what you would like," Adriana said. "It would have to be something small, that we could carry with us, and that we could give to every child."

Morgan sat up in bed and tapped a finger on her chin.

"I thought we should give shed rabbit fur," Adriana said. "It's pretty and soft, but — "

"I thought most children wouldn't like it," I said.

"Some would," Adriana snapped back.

Morgan giggled. "There might be something better - for children, that is. Hmmm. What about coins? You know, money."

"Money," Adriana repeated.

"Well that was easy," Morgan said, lying back down.

"Except, we don't know what money or coins are," Adriana said.

Morgan sat up again, and reached over to a wooden table beside her bed, opened a drawer, and brought out a small bag knotted at the top. She opened it, and poured some round metal objects into her hand. They were shiny in the moonlight.

"These are coins," she said. "Money."

"I can see why you'd want them," I said. "They're pretty."

"They're more than that," Morgan said. "We use them to buy things. I'm saving up for a new hairbrush."

Our faces went blank.

"When I have enough of them, I'm going to take these coins to the market and trade them."

"Oh. We trade, too. The olders of our village trade berries with the squirrels and feathers with the birds in winter," Adriana said. "But, we don't have any money to give."

We flew back to Stonewood that night a little sad. There, we ran into Tomas, a village older who also was one of Adriana's fairy watchers.

He could tell by our drooping wings and our faces that something was wrong, and invited us to his tree for tea.

Eleven: Fairy Dust

"Tell me now, what is it that troubles you?" Tomas asked as he brought us acorn caps of tea.

"I need money," Adriana said.

"Money, eh?" Tomas said. "I know of this thing. What do you want it for?"

"My quest," Adriana said.

"Ah, yes. I know of that, too. For the squirrels," Tomas said, nodding.

"And we met this human, named Morgan, who told us we could trade coins for the human children's teeth after they came out. But we don't have any coins and don't know how to get them. Do you?"

"What makes you think an old fairy like me would have coins?"

"I just..."

Tomas stood up very slowly from the table we were sitting around and shuffled over to an old sack on a shelf. He untied a knot at the top, and as he did, bits of dried vine like embers from a fire spread into the air.

He pulled out a scoop of glowing bright pink dust, filled a tiny acorn top from his pocket and brought it to Adriana.

"Fetch me a spoonful of water, please."

Adriana dipped a wooden spoon into a water barrel just outside the tree, and brought it.

Tomas told her to spread the water on the table, and then he sprinkled a few grains of the dust into the droplets.

Suddenly, the drops started to shiver. They shook faster and faster, until they went "pop!" and changed shape. The water had turned into coins — just like the ones Morgan had.

"How did you — ?"

Tomas smiled. "Fairy dust," he said. "It's magical. Are these coins like the ones you saw?"

"Yes, they're money," Adriana shrugged.

"Ah, yes, quite true. But this dust can change water into all kinds of different money," Tomas said. "Even money made from very thin pieces of wood."

"Wood?" Adriana asked.

"Made of wood," Tomas said. "Humans call it paper."

"Different money? I, I don't understand," she said.

"Have you heard the story of the Great Divide? Long ago, all of the world's creatures went their own way. Humans, too. Before the Great Divide they were all the same — looked and talked the same, ate the same foods, used the same money. And at that time, they all loved each other.

"But after the Great Divide, some of the humans made up new words for themselves and started to eat different foods. And many moons later, they began to even look different from one another. Later still, some of them forgot how to love those who were different," Tomas said. "So today, because of that, different humans have different money."

Shuffling back to the shelf, Tomas put a fistful of the colored dust into a small sack and handed it to Adriana.

"Here. For your quest," Tomas said. "I suppose I did have some money after all," he chuckled.

"Thanks be to you, Tomas," Adriana said, clapping her wings together. "I didn't know you could work such magic."

Tomas laughed again. "There is an old saying: Things with fairies are not always as they seem. But go now, and do what you must. I wish you good air."

We waved goodbye and flew off.

"Now we can trade the humans for their teeth," Adriana said to me. "Come on. We've only one full moon left."

Twelve: All About Teeth

For the next several moons, Adriana and I went from bedroom to bedroom, gathering teeth and leaving coins made from the magic dust Tomas gave us and water droplets we found on the grass.

Often the first shreds of light would be about when we returned to our forest, loaded down with teeth. We thought we nearly had enough for all the squirrels.

One night, after filling Adriana's satchel full, we visited Morgan. She told us something we hadn't thought of before.

"You have helped the village children more than I believe you could know," she said. "Having a tooth come out can be a little scary, at first. Do fairies lose their teeth?"

We shook our heads no.

"Well, sometimes there's a little bit of blood," Morgan said. "And if you're not used to that, that's hard. Also, a tooth is usually the first thing a human child loses in their lives, and that's even harder."

I tried to imagine what the squirrels felt.

"You've made the whole thing more fun," Morgan added. "And I've not met anyone who doesn't like a little money."

She sat up on her elbows.

"Word of you has spread to other villages, and those children want you to visit them, too. Could you? It would mean a lot to them. So you see, while you've been on a quest for your kind, you've also been doing something good for us humans."

Adriana smiled, but I could tell she was a little sad, too.

"I, I don't know when we'll see you again after tonight," she said. "Please know that we'll never forget you. You've helped us so much. From this moon on, Stonewood will speak of you as Morgan Fatata – Morgan of the fairies – because you are our friend."

"I'll never forget you, either," Morgan said. "Remember how I promised to tell you about human teeth? Would you like to learn now?"

We said we would, and Morgan told us all she knew about how human teeth grew, why they fell out and when, and how you had to clean them with a special brush and some stringy stuff at least two times every day.

When she finished, Adriana and I thanked her and kissed her cheeks. Her skin smelled sweet and her hair like flowers.

We turned to go.

"Adriana," Morgan said. "Can I tell other humans about you, and about your quest?"

Adriana said yes.

"Good. I want everyone to know about you, and what you're doing for the Black Squirrels in the name of friendship," Morgan said. "Just remember: You're close to the end, but your quest isn't finished quite yet."

If only we'd known then how right she was.

Thirteen: Midnight surprise

As we were leaving, Morgan told us about a boy whose family lived down the lane; they had very little money. She said he'd lost a tooth that very day and that he would be very happy if we visited his house.

We found his window cracked open. Inside, we could hear his soft breathing. The boy was sleeping so deeply that Adriana did not even bother to tap her necklace's purple stone after we'd made some money from dew on the grass.

She asked me if I wanted to come inside with her. I'd never seen Adriana actually collect a tooth, so I was excited to watch.

She glided down onto the boy's bed with a coin in each hand and wiggled under the pillow, like a caterpillar squirming under a leaf. I giggled, and flew to the bottom of the boy's bed to get a better view.

A few heartbeats later, she wiggled out backwards.

"Got it!" she said, holding up the tooth.

"And I've got you."

We spun around. Standing on the windowsill was a sprite about a strawberry taller than us, carrying a wooden sword made from a tree twig.

Adriana and I gasped.

"Sephian's my name," he said.

Olcas had told us about him. He said whenever Trench wanted something bad done, Sephian did it.

"Red Trench knows about your little tooth quest," he said. "He's not happy."

Sephian lifted his wooden sword and touched the point of it with a finger, before jumping in the air and flying after Adriana. He was faster than she was, and no matter how fast she dove, spun or darted around the boy's room, he stayed close behind her.

She ended up in a corner of the room's ceiling, panting. Sephian pulled up in front of her, trapping her.

I felt helpless, and too scared to move.

"When I catch you, I am going to tie you and your friend up with spider's silk, just as we did with the squirrels. Then I will take you to Trench," Sephian said, smiling.

"How does it feel to know that you have come so far, Adriana, and gotten so many teeth, only to have your quest fail?" Sephian asked her, laughing.

"I suppose," Adriana said, stopping and swallowing hard. "I suppose it feels..."

"Yes?"

"Well I suppose it would feel as you will, when you've failed," Adriana said calmly.

And with that, she tapped the purple stone on her necklace and disappeared.

Sephian jerked his head to the right, then to the left, looking for her. She was nowhere to be seen. To stop any escape, he flew to the windowsill and pushed the boy's window down. He then pulled a round piece of glass from a pocket, and held it to his eye.

"Ah, Adriana, there you are — on the bed next to your friend."

I didn't see Adriana at all.

"But...how?" I heard her say.

"With this," Sephian said, holding up the thick piece of glass. "I have magic, too, you see, and you have no powers left, Adriana. Try getting away from me now."

I looked about, trying to figure some way out. The room had two doors. One appeared to lead out to the house, but it was shut. The other was cracked open about a fairy height, but didn't look like it went outside.

"Give up?" Sephian asked.

"No," Adriana said. "You'll just have to catch me."

"I was hoping you'd say that," Sephian said. "More sporting for me that way."

A moment later, I felt a slight breeze beside me.

"Pilfria!" Adriana said in a loud whisper.

She was speaking backwards — like in our game!

"Anairda," I said. "Pilfria?" She wanted to play airflip — now?

"Pilfria!" she replied.

"What's that?" Sephian said, close enough to be

Adriana's shadow on a bright day.

Then I understood. The cracked door.

Sephian didn't pay any attention to me when I flew to a wall near it. He was too busy chasing Adriana.

From across the room, I could see Sephian swipe at the floor with his little sword and bolt towards me, the piece of glass still pressed against his one eye.

"Pilfria!" Adriana said again, louder this time, as she turned visible and flew into the dark crack.

Sephian was only the length of a long pine needle behind her. He was smiling a crooked smile.

He had trapped her — or so he thought.

In an eyeblink, Adriana came flying out. As she did, I flew with all my strength into the door and pushed it closed.

We heard Sephian thump against the hard wood. Adriana and I hugged in the air.

"You, you get me out of here, Adriana!" he said.

"He's about to take a long nap," Adriana said.

"Nap?"

"When I was in there flipping, I threw a handful of the sleepdust Olcas gave me into the air above me. It's probably all over him."

"I mean it, Adriana," came the voice from behind the door, followed by a loud, long yawn. "You'll set me free or you'll ... be ... sorry."

We could hear Sephian scratching the inside of the

door with his twig sword, and then the gentle sound of his breathing.

Together we opened the window. As we did, the human boy rolled over in his bed.

"I'd like to see Sephian's face when that human opens that door," I said.

"I'd like to see that human's face when he sees Sephian!" Adriana replied.

We laughed about it all the way back to Stonewood.

Fourteen: Red Trench Comes Back

The moon was filling up again in the night sky. We wanted to test our plan to give the squirrels new teeth before it did.

Olcas agreed to melt down a few of the children's teeth with a spell, but only because we followed him around the village for most of a morning, asking him over and over again if he would.

After they were melted, we put them in wooden shells we'd made shaped like the squirrel's teeth, and waited for them to harden.

Kliren agreed to try them, and Olcas' helper Valandoor used juniper berries and garlic to make a glue so they'd stay put.

Once inside his mouth, the Black Squirrel felt his new teeth with his small hands, and smiled.

He let a loud squawk of approval, which made all the other squirrels chirp and swish their tails in the trees. We planned to get to work on the other new squirrel teeth with the very next sun.

"We have just about enough children's teeth for every squirrel," Adriana said. "We just need to get a few more."

But we wouldn't have the chance. During the very

next dark, we awoke to the squirrels' squawking.

We knew what the noise meant: Red Trench was coming.

His crows flew in first, swooping in from above with sharp, hooked beaks and eyes filled with hate.

We all got together under an oak tree and stood close to one another, too scared to move.

Outside our village, we could see animals marching toward us, led by Trench and Sephian. I could see rats, bugs, scorpions and snakes. Suddenly, Trench stopped just outside Stonewood. All the animals and bugs did, too.

"It's been three full moons," Trench called out. "I warned you. Join me to defeat the giants, or else... What say you, fairies of Stonewood?"

Olcas was not among us, and the rest of us were too scared to say anything.

Trench turned around to face his army.

"Get them all!"

And with that, the snakes slithered, the rats ran, the bugs scurried and the scorpions crawled, all toward us.

We all ran or flew as fast as we could, careful to stay away from the crows.

I made for a large tree, half flying, half running. Adriana was just behind me, but she slipped and fell. In an eyeblink, Sephian was standing over her.

"I told you I'd get you," he said.

Sephian reached out to grab Adriana, but as he did, she quickly jumped up and flew about a branch length away. Before he had a chance to catch her, an owl swooped down, grabbed Sephian in its sharp feet, and flew silently off.

We looked up. Called by the squirrels, a great pack of eagles and owls had flown in to help us.

The owls chased the crows away, and several eagles made a big circle around us. Seeing the birds, Trench's army turned and left our village in a hurry. A pair of owls chased them, flying low to the ground, to make sure they stayed away.

We all cheered, and hugged.

Suddenly, Adriana noticed a light coming from inside Olcas' tree. She went to it, and found him sitting at a small table, bent over and with his back to her.

"Olcas," she said. "I am so happy to see you!"

"Is it over?" he asked, without turning.

"Yes," Adriana said. "Eagles and owls came to our rescue. Trench ran way."

Olcas breathed deeply.

"I tried to help."

"We know you did, Olcas, but Trench — "

"I tried to make Stonewood see," he went on. "But now, we will all be lost forever."

"Lost?"

"To the humans, of course!" he said, his voice rising as he turned to face her. "They will take this whole land. Soon there will be no safe place for fairies. You've seen yourself how they cut the trees! Soon we will be nothing more than a part of their stories."

"But, I've met a human," Adriana said. "She helped with the tooth quest. She's my friend. They're not all bad."

"Not all bad?" he laughed. "And you and your quest! I counted on Gram to eat you, and Sephian to make sure you didn't leave that human house. But they both failed. Do you know what you've done?"

"Gram? Sephian? What?" Adriana said, shaking her head.

Olcas waved his arm from the top of his head downward to his stomach, and when he finished, he had turned into Red Trench.

"Surprised, Adriana? I had to do this to show Stonewood how bad the humans are. It was the only way."

"Things with fairies really are not always as they seem," Adriana whispered to herself.

Trench stepped closer to Adriana. "I was trying to save us! Together, we could have pushed the humans from our forest."

"But, you, I mean, Olcas, you gave me the necklace."

"I made sure the necklace wouldn't work with every human when I made it," he said, stepping in front of the doorway to his tree. "I was counting on you to be caught — not make a friend!"

He moved his hand from his stomach up to his head again, and turned back into Olcas. He then raised his hands above his head, the way he did just before casting a spell.

"Olcas Dona Sufartach!" a voice shouted behind him. It was Kliren. "What is the meaning of this?"

The black squirrel stood upright, and flashed his new front teeth at Olcas.

"I, well … "Kliren, look!" Olcas said, pointing.

The squirrel turned, just long enough for Olcas to dart by him and fly away into the night.

"Adriana," Kliren said. "Are you alright?"

"I, I think I will be. Thanks be to you, Kliren." She hugged him, as he put his small hands on her shoulders.

Adriana walked out of Olcas' tree and sunk to the ground. We gathered around her and gently touched her wings to comfort her.

"Trench is gone," I whispered.

"So is Olcas," Adriana said. "We were all tricked. Olcas and Trench were one and the same. And now no one knows how to work the magic to melt all the children's teeth we collected for the rest of the squirrels."

But then a small voice called out.

"There is someone," the voice said.

It was Valandoor.

"I, I know that I am, was, only Olcas' helper, but I watched him very closely, and learned a little magic. I'll try to melt those teeth for you."

None of us had ever heard Valandoor say so many words at one time.

Adriana smiled.

We set to work straight away. Valandoor turned the first batch of teeth he tried to melt into flowers, but after that, he got it right.

By the next sun, they were ready. We worked together to fit them into the squirrels' mouths.

"The quest is finally over," I said to Adriana as we sat together on a tree branch watching the sunset, after all the squirrels had been taken care of.

"No," Adriana said. "'Tis not."

"What? Of course it is. Trench is gone, and the squirrels have teeth again."

"I've been thinking about the human children," Adriana said. "You heard what Morgan said. Losing a tooth can be scary for humans. We helped, and can help still. Morgan said there were other villages, other children. Remember?"

I did.

I looked at her then, and saw how much she'd grown since the quest began. She was no longer the little fairy who was scared of her own shadow. She'd outsmarted Gram the fox, made friends with Morgan, escaped Sephian and beaten Red Trench. I knew that the next steps in her journey she could take on her own.

We hugged long and hard, and I wished her good air.

Adriana put on the Necklace of Secrets, slung her tooth satchel with Tomas' fairy dust in it over her shoulder, and dove off the tree branch. But before flying away, she stopped and turned back to me.

"Can you do me a favor?"

"Anything," I said.

"I think I'm going to need a bigger satchel," Adriana said.

"I'll make you one myself," I said, smiling.

And with that, Adriana — the Tooth Fairy — set off for the human villages once more.

THE END *(For Now)*

Made in the USA
Charleston, SC
20 January 2017